P9-DMW-900

Marilyn Janovitz

THREE LITTLE KITTENS

A CHESHIRE STUDIO BOOK

NORTH-SOUTH BOOKS · NEW YORK · LONDON

Three little kittens,

they lost their mittens

and they began to cry,

"Oh, mother dear, we sadly fear
that we have lost our mittens."

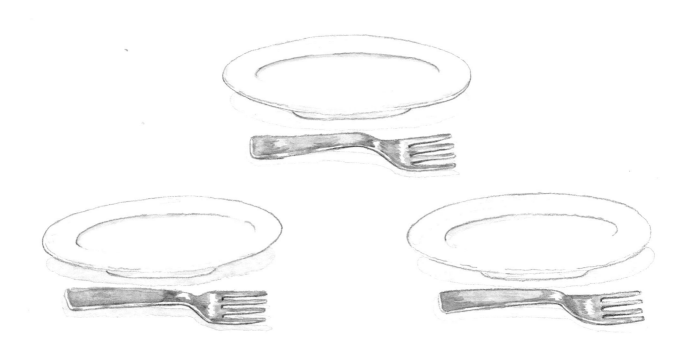

"What! Lost your mittens,
you naughty kittens!
Then you shall have no pie."
Meow, meow, meow, meow.
"No, you shall have no pie."

The three little kittens,

they found their mittens,

and they began to cry,
"Oh, mother dear, see here, see here,
for we have found our mittens."

"Put on your mittens, you silly kittens,
and you shall have some pie."
Purrr, purrr, purrr, purrr.
"Oh, let us have some pie."

The three little kittens
put on their mittens,

and soon ate up the pie.

"Oh, mother dear, we greatly fear
that we have soiled our mittens."
"What! Soiled your mittens,
you naughty kittens!"
Then they began to sigh.
Meow, meow, meow, meow.
Then they began to sigh.

The three little kittens,
they washed their mittens,

and hung them out to dry.

"Oh, mother dear, do you not hear
that we have washed our mittens?"
"What! Washed your mittens,
then you're good little kittens!

But I smell a rat close by."

Meow, meow, meow, meow.

"We smell a rat close by."

FOR CHERYL AND ANTHONY

Illustrations copyright © 2002 by Marilyn Janovitz
All rights reserved. No part of this book may be reproduced or utilized in any form
or by any means, electronic or mechanical, including photocopying, recording, or any
information storage and retrieval system, without permission in writing from the publisher.

A CHESHIRE STUDIO BOOK
Published in the United States by North-South Books Inc., New York.
Published simultaneously in Great Britain, Canada, Australia, and
New Zealand in 2002 by North-South Books, an imprint
of Nord-Süd Verlag AG, Gossau Zürich, Switzerland.

Library of Congress Cataloging-in-Publication Data is available.
The CIP catalogue record for this book is available from The British Library.

ISBN 0-7358-1642-5 (trade edition)
1 3 5 7 9 HC 10 8 6 4 2
ISBN 0-7358-1643-3 (library edition)
1 3 5 7 9 LE 10 8 6 4 2
Printed in Hong Kong

For more information about our books, and the authors and artists
who create them, visit our web site: www.northsouth.com

PEACHTREE

J 398.8 JANOVITZ

Janovitz, Marilyn.
   Three little kittens

OCT 0 8 2002

Atlanta-Fulton Public Library